DONNIE'S DANGER

Written by Aleda Renken
Illustrated by Art Kirchhoff

A Haley Adventure Book

Publishing House
St. Louis

To Steve with love

Copyright © 1981 by Concordia Publishing House
3558 South Jefferson Avenue, St. Louis, MO 63118

Library of Congress Cataloging in Publication Data

Renken, Aleda.
    Donnie's danger.

    (Her A Haley adventure book)
    SUMMARY: Six-year-old Donnie longs for a real
"adventure" but when he finally gets one, he is none too
happy with the experience.
    [1. Christian life—Fiction. I. Title.
PZ7.R289Do   [Fic]   80-22721
ISBN 0-570-07235-2

1 2 3 4 5 6 7 8 9 10 CB 90 89 88 87 86 85 84 83 82 81

CHAPTER 1

"How old do you have to be before you can have an adventure?" six-year-old Donnie asked his older brother, as they picked up fallen rotten apples and tossed them into a big barrel.

Jeff picked up the apples carefully, because of bees that gathered around them, and Jeff had had some bad experiences in being too chummy with bees.

"You can ask the dumbest questions. Do you think you have to send in an application for an adventure when you get to be a certain age?"

"All the kids in our family and Sam, our neighbor, have had exciting adventures, but I've never had one—not ever."

"I admit that picking up apples isn't fun, but if we don't get them cleaned up it means an adventure with Mom or Dad."

Donnie looked up at the branches drooping low with apples.

"This tree is crazy. Any tree this old has no business having so many apples. We don't know what to do with them. Mom, Pat, and Granny have made jars and jars of jelly and applesauce. Besides, every day we've been

5

eating apple pie, or apple dumplings, or fried apples, or baked apples, or apple cake, apple pudding, and—"

Jeff broke in. "And you know what? I heard Granny telling Mom that she had just heard about a recipe with apples that made catsup."

"Oh, no! The worst of it is that we don't have time to do anything else. I haven't had a chance to practice my pitching at all," Donnie complained.

"You'll never be any good pitching anyway. I watched you last week. You can't even hit the side of a barn."

"I can too. Look—" Donnie got off his knees, picked up an apple, wound up, and threw hard. His apple hit the barn and ended up a big squashed brown spot. "I told you I could," Donnie shrieked.

"Just pure luck."

"Then you do it—go on."

Jeff picked up an apple, wound up, and threw hard. His apple also ended up on the barn—a big rotten spot.

Not to be outdone—or equalled—Donnie tried it again and again and hit the side of the barn every time. He shouted with glee. Jeff thought it was much more fun hitting the barn than throwing the spoiled apples into a barrel. They were having a great time until their mother came outside. She frowned at the spotted barn.

"That settles it. No swimming for either of you this afternoon. After you get all the apples picked up, you will hose down the side of the barn. I'm disgusted! We don't like our job inside the hot kitchen either, but we aren't throwing jam at the kitchen wall."

The screen door slammed, and the boys began picking up apples and throwing them into the barrel that would be trucked to Mr. Harrison's hog pen.

"I wish someone would do something about this crazy tree," Donnie grumbled.

"Like what? You can't shoot a tree. Would you suggest dynamite? Remember, this tree is going about its business of having fruit for us for the long winter—"

Their sister Pat came outside. She wiped the sweat off her face with her shirttail.

"We're going to stop for today. As soon as Sam and Kurt come home we'll go for a swim. Too bad you two clowns had to decorate the barn." She gazed at the brown spots drying to a hard crust on the barn. "Wow! That stuff is going to be hard to get off."

Granny followed Pat out of the kitchen. She wasn't really the Haley's grandmother. She was their neighbor and the grandmother of Sam, but the Haley children and their parents loved her as much as if she belonged to them.

She looked at the tree and shook her head. "We've canned and jellied and baked and cooked apples for the past two days, and this tree is still loaded."

"Why can't they just go to waste in peace?" Donnie asked, looking around the grass to be sure they had picked up all the fallen apples. "Or why can't we send them to the starving kids in all those awful countries where they don't have apple trees?"

Just then a big ripe apple plopped hard on his head. It squashed to a brown mess and juice ran down his forehead into his eyes.

Pat turned her back to hide the big grin on her face, but Granny didn't crack a smile.

"Of course we can't let them go to waste," Mrs. Haley said, coming out of the door. The good Lord gave us all this fruit, and it's stuffed with vitamins, and we're going to love eating them next winter."

Just then, Kurt, the oldest Haley boy, and Sam, the neighbor, came around to the back of the house. They had been helping Sam's dad cut and bale hay, and they were stripped to cutoff jeans. Bits of hay stuck to their sweaty skin.

"Now for a swim," Kurt said. "You guys ready?" He looked at his younger brother. "What are you doing, Donnie? Are you trying out a new apple-shampoo? Now that's another way we could use apples—right, Granny?"

But Granny didn't answer. She had come

outside to look thoughtfully at the roof of the Haley house. At the top of the grey rock house there was a flat place.

Kurt followed her look. "What's up there? Granny? Santa Claus coming down the chimney?"

"I've got an idea. Is there a way to get up to that place at the top of the house? It looks nice and flat." She talked fast, as she always did when she had a bright idea.

"Yeah. You can crawl out of the bathroom window and then put up a stepladder against the wall and climb to the level part. I helped Dad mend the roof one time, so I know," Kurt said.

"Then that's it," Granny said, nodding her gray head. "No jars, no jelly glasses, no heat—Ruth!" she called.

"I'm inside, Granny. I'm closing up the kitchen so I can turn on the air conditioning. I'll never be able to cook supper if I don't get it cooled off. What do you want?"

"I've got an idea," Granny said and went into the kitchen. They didn't hear the rest of what she said and really didn't care.

Kurt looked at his friend Sam. "I think someone we both love has flipped her piazza. What can apples have to do with the flat part of our roof?"

"You can stay and find out. I'm headed for the river before someone finds me another job." Sam broke into a run and headed for the

9

path that led through the woods to a deep quiet pool under the willows on the river. Kurt followed right behind him.

"Wait for me," Pat called but didn't really expect the boys to sit around and wait until she put on her bathing suit.

Jeff and Donnie looked mournfully at each other and then at the spotted barn. They went to hook up the hose so it would reach to the barn.

Mrs. Haley and Granny came outside and stood gazing at the roof.

"My mother used to dry apples all the time. And were they ever delicious! They were especially good in fried pies—or tarts. We won't need heat in the kitchen at all. All we have to do is quarter them and put them in buckets. We'll put ropes on the bucket handles, and the boys can pull them up on the roof. We can hose off all those discarded screens you stored in the barn, and they can pull them up too. Then the two big boys can spread the quartered apples on the screens, and the sun will do the rest."

"Sounds wonderful," Mrs. Haley said doubtfully.

"What if it rains?" Donnie asked. The roof looked awfully far up to Donnie He hated looking down and was glad that he was the smallest Haley kid and wouldn't be asked to go up and spread apples on screens to dry.

"It won't. We're in the dry period now. It

hasn't rained for three weeks, and the weather man says there's no chance for any rain for at least a week. By that time the apples will be all dried and ready to be stored for the winter."

Mrs. Haley looked at the two boys dragging the long hose toward the barn.

"You may take a short break, boys, before you start to clean the barn wall. There's a pitcher of lemonade in the kitchen."

Donnie and Jeff got big glasses of the chilled drink and went to a small rise in the lawn where the back yard turned into the front yard.

Jeff moved away from Donnie as they sat in the shade of the big oak.

"You smell like a rotten apple."

"That tree threw that apple on my head because I've been talking mean about it," said Donnie as he looked back at the tree. "I know one thing—I won't eat any of those apples they say they're going to dry on the roof."

"Donnie, you make me tired. You always think it's important what you like and why not—"

"It *is* important. You know why?"

"Go ahead, you'll tell me anyhow."

"Flies!" Donnie said dramatically. "What's going to keep a hundred million flies from coming down from the manure pile up in Sam's dad's cattle yard? They'll walk around on

those apples with all their dirty feet—and how many feet do flies have?"

"That's something to think about," Jeff said, gazing up at the roof,"—not how many feet they have, but how high does a fly fly? Would they fly that high?"

"We could find out," Donnie said eagerly. "We could sit on the—" but suddenly his voice lost sound. "Never mind. Skip it. I wouldn't want to sit way up there watching for flies."

"You're too chicken," Jeff said, putting his empty glass down and lying back in the sweet cool clover.

"I'm *not* chicken."

"Yes you are, and that's why you aren't having any adventures. You've got to be willing to do new things." Jeff got up and started toward the hose and the barn.

Donnie followed him. He was shouting. "I'm going to have the best adventure anyone in the world ever had. You just wait and see."

The two boys found out that rotten apples stick like glue if a ninety degree sun bakes down on them. By the time Pat and the two big boys came back from their swim, Jeff and Donnie had just finished cleaning off the last big glob of mushy brown apple from the barn wall.

All through the evening Donnie was so quiet that Mrs. Haley noticed it and felt his head to see if he had a fever.

"He's not sick," Jeff said in disgust," he's just trying to think up an adventure."

"Think up an adventure?" Pat turned to look at her little brother. "Are you going to write stories?"

"Jeff, I wish you wouldn't always blab everything I say," Donnie said angrily.

"It's really nothing to be ashamed of," Jeff said quickly. "You see, Donnie thinks everyone in the family has had an adventure except him."

"But you did have one. Remember the convict in the cave? That was a real honest-to-goodness adventure," Pat consoled him.

"This is ridiculous talk. Stop teasing Donnie. Listen, dear. I haven't had an adventure either and I'm having a very happy life. I'm satisfied just o—" Mrs. Haley broke off because the telephone rang.

Kurt jumped up to answer it. He came back. "It's for you, Mom," he said then he turned to his little brother.

"Tell you what. If we're going to put apples on the roof to dry, like Granny said, then you can be the guy to do it. You'll probably slip, and then you can hang on the side of the roof with your teeth—no, two of the front ones are gone—you can hang with your chewed-off fingernails. Now *that* would be an adventure. We'd have a guy from the local paper take

14

pictures," Kurt spoke softly. His mother was talking excitedly over the telephone.

"I think you and Jeff are being hateful," Pat began but looked up to see her mother come into the room. Mrs. Haley had an odd expression on her face.

"I can't believe it," she said, sinking into the big armchair.

"I know what you can't believe," Jeff laughed, "that someone wants to give us twenty bushels of nice apples."

"Just what we need," Kurt chuckled. "Tell them to bring them right out and dump them under the old apple tree and then—"

"Will you two please be quiet and let Mom tell us what she can't believe," Pat demanded.

"I'm supposed to go to San Francisco the day after tomorrow," Mrs. Haley shook her head as if the words she had said didn't quite sink into her brain.

The boys stopped laughing, and both said together, "San Francisco!"

Mrs. Haley began to talk in a slow, dazed voice. "This spring the Ladies Auxiliary decided to pay all expenses to send a delegate to San Francisco for the national convention. Mrs. Douglas offered to go, and they voted on her because she has no family and can always get away. Before I knew it—because I was on the serving committee that day—they named me as alternate. I didn't protest, because I was sure

Mrs. Douglas would go—there's nothing ever happens to her—thank God," she said quickly and sincerely.

"And now something *has* happened to her?" Pat prompted.

"Yes, she fell off a ski at the lake yesterday and broke her leg. So now—" her voice faded away.

"So now you're going to get a chance to go to San Francisco for free. I'm sorry Mrs. Douglas broke her leg, but I'm glad you got a chance to get away for a little while. You need to," Granny said happily.

Mrs. Haley looked frightened. "But I can't. I've a family to look after and these—these crazy apples shouldn't be wasted," there was a half-sob in her voice.

"Mom, you surely don't mean you'd let an overproductive apple tree keep you from going on a free trip to San Francisco?" Kurt shouted.

"I'll take good care of your family, child, and love it. And we'll not waste the apples either. Now, you must take this trip."

"Mom, it's your chance for adventure," said Donnie as he jumped up and down in excitement. "You've *got* to go, or it might be your last chance to have an adventure. You're not so young anymore."

"But day after tomorrow—it's impossible to get ready by that time." Mrs. Haley got up with a grim expression on her face. "I'm calling the president of the auxiliary. She'll *have* to find someone else."

"Please, please talk to Dad first. See what he has to say," Pat begged.

Mrs. Haley hesitated, "Granny, would you really move in here for four or five days?"

"I'd be tickled to death to have a change. Sam can sleep at home and eat his meals here—he does most of the time anyway."

Mrs. Haley left to go to the telephone, and suddenly it hit Donnie that he would have to be without his mother for almost a week.

"How will she get all that far away?" he was really thinking out loud.

"Oxen and covered wagon," Kurt laughed.

"By jet," Jeff looked wistfully out at the blue expanse of summer sky. "It's wonderful. I'll never forget our flight to Padre Island, will you, guys?"

"No, I won't. I also remember you sitting there holding the puke-bag," Sam chuckled.

"Shame on you for talking that way, Sam," Granny scolded, but her eyes twinkled.

Mrs. Haley came in with her face flushed and her eyes sparkling.

"Dad said he'd be angry if I passed up this opportunity. He's coming home right now. He says there's nothing doing at the office anyway, and he'll take me shopping. Pat, please run that basket of wash through the washer, and—oh, my, my—" she was running out of breath.

That night, after adding a petition to his prayers to give his mother a safe journey, Donnie looked uncertainly at his big sister who was taking his mother's place at the prayer session.

"You did finish?—or do you want to add something?" she asked.

"You think God would mind me asking for just one little adventure?" he asked timidly.

"I think God and all His angels have much more important things to do than plan silly adventures for a spoiled kid who should be thankful he has such a nice life."

"But I thanked for that already. Besides, with all those bad things going on in the world, like riots and people setting fires and earthquakes and—"

"People don't set earthquakes" Pat broke in.

"No, but there are robberies and bombs for them to tend to—the angels I mean. Maybe it would be a nice change for them to plan a nice adventure, like Mom getting away from us and the apples."

Pat got up and turned off the light.

"I'm not listening to that kind of junk. Good night."

18

CHAPTER 2

The day that Mrs. Haley left for San Francisco Granny called the kids together for a meeting. They sat under the crazy apple tree and tried to avoid making the busy bees angry. Even Poochie, Donnie's pup, attended the meeting and listened politely to every word that was said.

Kurt thought that Granny sounded a lot like a coach before a football game.

"We're not going to let this tree get the best of us. By noon I don't want any apples left on this tree, except those too high for us to reach. We're going to *dry* apples. Kurt, you and Sam make a dry-run up to the roof and see if we can put screen trays of apples out on the flat part of the roof. Be very careful! No apples are worth one of you breaking a leg."

"Come on, Sam," Kurt yelled gleefully. He was always happy doing new and exciting things.

Before Granny could say more, both boys had disappeared into the house. Soon they were climbing out of the small bathroom window.

"Hey," Kurt shouted, "we need the ladder

19

to get to the top. Pat, you and Jeff and Donnie can drag it up from the barn. We'll pull it up and put it on the wall, so we can reach the flat part of the roof."

"We always get the dirty work," Donnie grumbled.

"*You* want to climb to the roof?" Pat demanded, and Donnie said no more.

As soon as they had dragged the ladder to the house wall, Sam and Kurt pulled it up and leaned it against the wall that went to the high flat part. When the two boys got up to that part, they gave a few wild yelps and a dance that they thought was Indian. Granny came outside and shouted for them to stop being so reckless.

"Jeff, you tie ropes on the buckets and screens as the boys lower the ropes. Pat, you fill the buckets with quartered apples. Jeff, hose down the screens and tie them on the ropes. With all of us working we should be done by noon."

And they were.

The Haley children and Sam were free for the afternoon and made plans for baseball and tennis—all except Donnie, who was considered too young for anything except swimming—and that only with Pat or the big boys around to watch him.

So, in the cheerful sitting room Granny took off her shoes and settled herself in her favorite rocker at the Haley house for a snooze.

The big house was fairly cool, even without air conditioning. A breeze blew in the sweetness of newly cut grass and sun-drenched hay.

Donnie got out his favorite game—a wooden box with his collection of small cars. It also had a small ramp made out of boards. He played races. But mostly he listened to Granny snore.

Granny was very fancy with her snoring. Each snore had a different sound and a different rhythm. Why did people snore only when they were asleep? Was there a button somewhere inside their brain that turned itself on when someone was asleep? And why snore at all? Was it to scare robbers away or make them feel safe? Well, it was none of his business. God made people to snore when they were asleep, and Donnie knew that He had a reason for it.

Donnie was a little ashamed how he had bothered God for an adventure. He hoped that God or His special angels might not have been listening. But he figured that it was no big sin to at least ask.

He raced the yellow car and the red car down the ramp, but like always, the red car turned over, and the yellow one won. It was boring. Even his toy cars couldn't do anything exciting. He put away his cars to go outside and play hide-and-seek with Poochie. His dog was just beginning to catch on to the game.

It was just as he closed the box with the

small cars that he heard a rumble. It wouldn't be thunder, because the weather man said it wouldn't rain for at least another week. But, just to be sure, he ran to the front door and saw black clouds boiling up far to the west.

"Granny, he shouted, "it's going to rain."

Granny woke with a start and gazed around in a daze.

"The apples that are supposed to dry will get wet," said Donnie as he ran to the front door again and saw a flash of lightning slice through the black clouds. Right afterwards came a crash of thunder. Poochie howled at the front door, and Donnie let him in.

Granny shook her head to get rid of the dreams she had been having. "Get the boys. We've got to get those apples down, or they'll all be ruined."

"I can't get the boys, Granny, they are way over at Graham's pasture, playing baseball. Pat's in town playing tennis with some girls."

"Oh, my, my!" Granny sat down again to pull on her shoes. "We'll have to get those apples down ourselves, honey."

"You mean *climb on the roof*?" Donnie gasped in horror.

Granny was hobbling toward the steps. Granny always hobbled after she had been sitting for a long time.

"We ain't got an elevator, have we?" Granny asked.

Donnie ran to the front door, hoping that somehow those clouds had all blown away. But there they were, looking worse than ever. Donnie wanted to crawl under a bed like he knew Poochie had done.

"Donnie," Granny called from upstairs. How had she hobbled up there so fast? "Come on, I can't get those apples in the buckets all by myself. I've got two buckets. You bring the other with rope on it. We'll soon have them under cover before the storm breaks."

Donnie saw the two buckets that stood right outside the kitchen door. Might as well take them both. He would look better if he fell down with two buckets rather than one. There was a scary stillness outside—not a leaf moved. He saw a little bird disappear inside a thick spruce tree. That bird had sense. Above him was that awful churning of tree tops and of clouds that seemed inside the trees. There was a moan of wind and rumble of thunder. Funny, the wind hadn't gotten down to the ground yet.

"Donnie, hurry," Granny yelled, and Donnie commanded his feet to carry him upstairs. He pushed the buckets through the bathroom window. Granny was climbing the ladder that led to the upper roof.

Donnie looked at the little bathroom window and worried that he could not get through it. Should he tell Granny that his stomach was too fat? No! Jeff and Kurt would tease him for the rest of his life. He stepped on the toilet stool and got one knee on the high window sill. He shoved his head and chest out of the opening then sucked in his stomach, held his breath, and pushed.

He got through.

Granny was already up on the flat roof and was scooping up apples and putting them in the buckets.

Donnie didn't have to look up to see the clouds. He was *in* them. The wind was wild. It billowed Granny's full dress like it was wired. She was on her hands and knees, picking up apples as fast as any machine could have done.

Donnie felt the wind tear at him as he climbed the ladder.

"We're going to be blown off the roof," he screamed, but Granny either didn't hear him or believe him. She kept on picking up little bits of half-withered apples like they were gold nuggets.

Donnie had just taken his foot off the top rung of the ladder, when a big powerful gust of wind whirled the ladder as though it was made of straw. He watched it as it was flung down on the roof below him.

"Don't just stand there," Granny shrieked. "Come on, put apples in your buckets."

"It's no use. The ladder just blew down. We're stuck up here," Donnie yelled above the roar of the wind.

Granny didn't stop scooping apples in her buckets. "Guess we'll have to jump," she yelled cheerfully.

But Donnie knew it was much too far for them to jump. It was even too far for guys like Kurt and Sam—and certainly for Granny, who must be at least a hundred years old.

"Fill your buckets," Granny ordered.

Then, with a heavy blackness, came the rain riding in on the wind. Donnie hadn't picked up one sliver of apple. The wind carried most of them far away. Water splashed in the buckets like into a river or swimming pool.

"Guess we might as well go down and leave the apples," Granny pushed plasters of wet hair from her eyes.

"I told you—we can't go down, because the wind blew the ladder flat on the kitchen roof. We're stuck up here." Donnie didn't know if it was worth crying about or not. He certainly didn't like his wet clothes pasted to him.

Granny crawled to the edge of the roof and saw the ladder far below in a puddle of water.

"I guess we can't jump. It sure would hurt my arthritis. Come on, we'll sit near the chimney and keep some of the wind off us."

So they huddled by the chimney, but the wind and rain hit them there too.

Donnie had always loved rainy nights when he was in bed and could hear the patter of raindrops on the roof and windowpanes, but the raindrops that day did not patter—they stung and slashed and beat.

Donnie turned to look at Granny. Rain was running in every wrinkle, and her hair was stuck in wet strings on her head and face. But her eyes were serene, and Donnie was ashamed of the few tears he had let mix with the raindrops.

"Here's your adventure, honey," Granny shouted above the noise of the storm.

"This is no real adventure," Donnie yelled. "We aren't hanging from a cliff or just about to be chewed up by a shark."

"But we could be struck by lightning—" before she could finish her sentence there was a frightning crack, and then the thunder came, and they heard a loud splintering noise from somewhere below them.

"What was that?" Donnie was wondering if he had been struck by lightning and didn't know it.

Granny shook her head, leaning back against the chimney. Donnie wondered if she were asleep and snoring. Soon the rain slowed down and the wind was not so strong. Granny got up with a groan, her bones creaking. She limped carefully across the slippery roof.

"Well, that's that!" she said. Donnie got up and joined her and saw that she was looking down at the overbearing apple tree. The tree had

split in two, and limbs and apples lay scattered far and wide.

They heard a motor just then and started toward the front of the roof. Mr. Head, their mailman, came around the curve of the road in his old car.

"Flag him down," Granny said quickly.

Carefully Donnie got down on his hands and knees and crawled to the edge of the front roof. He lay flat on his stomach and waited until the car stopped by the mail box and then he shouted.

"Mr. Head!"

The little fat man had just shoved some mail in their box and slammed it shut. He looked around uncertainly, trying to find out where the voice came from.

"Up here, on the roof," Donnie cried.

Mr. Head looked up and his eyes bulged when he saw Granny and Donnie's soaked heads peeping over the edge of the dripping roof.

"What in the name of sense?" he muttered.

"We came up here to save some apples, young man," Granny said, although Donnie was sure that Mr. Head was as old as Granny.

"Save apples?" It was too much for poor Mr. Head to understand.

"Would you be kind enough to walk in the house and up the stairs and into the bathroom? Then, if you'll climb out of the bathroom window you will see a fallen ladder. Please put it against the roof. Then Donnie and I can get down and dry out. Now that doesn't have anything to do with carrying mail, but it would be a nice thing for Uncle Sam to do for good patriotic people."

"Walk in the house—climb out the bath-room window—" said Mr. Head in a daze.

"Right. And would you mind to hurry? It's cold up here when you're soaked to the skin like we are and the wind is blowing."

Mr. Head started to the house, muttering feebly to himself.

"I do believe he's going to do it," Granny said and went to where the ladder would be replaced. "I'll certainly write Washington, D.C. and tell them what a nice thing our mailman did."

Soon they saw Mr. Head's flushed face at the bathroom window. He was shaking his head. "I'd sure like to help you, mam, but I couldn't begin to get through that window. But—maybe—maybe—I'll tell you what I'll do."

"You better go on a diet, that's what. What can you do for us?" Granny said sharply. She said in a whisper to Donnie. "I saw him at our last church supper. He eats like a pig."

But Mr. Head was talking. "The next house I come to I'll call in and have them send out the police with some ladders and they'll get you down."

"Don't you *dare.*" Granny roared. "How

will that look in the Auxiliary News Letter? Go on, deliver your mail and try to keep your mouth shut, although I don't think you will."

Mr. Head's face disappeared and soon they saw him trudge to his car, shaking his head and looking up at them as though he was glad to be getting away.

"He never did like me," Granny grumbled. "And I'll bet he tells everyone on his route about us up here."

"Never mind, Granny. Look, here comes Kurt and Sam," Donnie cried, waving his arms wildly.

Kurt and Sam acted like it was the most natural thing in the world to get a soaked Granny and Donnie off the roof. They grinned when they saw the apple tree, although by that time Donnie thought it was kind of sad. After all, the apple tree was just doing what apple trees are supposed to do.

Sam picked up a fairly sound apple and took a big juicy bite. "Your mother will hate this," he said.

"Next year she will—not this year," Kurt said.

"I hate loosing all those half-dry apples but I guess we have to pay something for Donnie's adventure," Granny said, heading for the kitchen door.

"That wasn't an adventure," Donnie said after the kitchen door slammed behind her.

"What *is* an adventure?" Sam asked.

"It's when you are in danger and someone loves you."

"We love you, Donnie," Kurt said but Donnie glared at him and dripped his way into the house.

In his prayers that night Donnie surprised Pat by adding a soft postscript to his other prayers.

"I guess I should thank you for that baby-adventure," he said almost in a whisper.

Donnie hadn't thought Pat would hear it but she said quickly, "What do you mean, 'baby-adventure'?"

"It wasn't really a honest-to-goodness adventure—where someone could—could *die.*"

Pat was horrified. "Honestly, Donnie Haley, I think you've gone beserk on this adventure business. I just hope you never regret saying that."

Donnie felt a little uneasy, but not enough to keep him awake. But he was to remember those words later.

CHAPTER 3

"How could one person away from her family leave such a big hole?" Donnie wondered as he climbed into bed. He'd certainly be glad when his mother came home—although Granny did have more caramel sauce on her apple dumplings than his mother.

Mrs. Haley called that evening from San Francisco and told their dad that she was excited and happy. She said she was having a wonderful adventure and would tell them about it when she got home.

Donnie kicked off the blanket. Why was he either too hot or too cold? Surely his mother being away couldn't be causing that. He wondered what her adventure had been. He had doubts that his mother even knew what an adventure was. He guessed he wouldn't have an adventure until he was old. He might even be twenty, and then there wouldn't be anyone around who knew him except real old people.

Pat came in. She was in her housecoat and had those funny rollers that looked like small sewer pipes in her hair. It was too bad Pat had to wear them just to try to be pretty. Girls were dumb!

Pat had had her bath and was ready to hear his prayers. When would she leave him alone to pray? Why couldn't God and he have a chance to talk between themselves?

"I can say my prayers without you," he said crossly.

"I know you can—if you don't fall asleep. But I promised Mom I would hear your prayers and I'm sticking to that. So, get going because I'm awfully tired."

So Donnie said his usual prayers with an extra one for his mother so far away. Then he hesitated.

"You finished?" Pat asked.

"This is going to be a private prayer," Donnie informed her. "I don't see why I can't say something to God without you sitting there and telling me what to say."

Pat got off the side of the bed. "You certainly can. I'll leave. But I hope you aren't going to bother God with something dumb."

"It's not whether *you* think it's dumb. It's whether He thinks it dumb—and I guess He's awfully used to dumb prayers."

"OK," Pat yawned and went to the door. "Sleep well, honey," she muttered as she went down the hall.

Kurt and Jeff were in their room sitting at their study table. Jeff was deep in a history book, but Kurt had heard Donnie's prayer because their room was just across the hall.

Kurt slammed his book so hard that his brother jumped.

Jeff looked up. "What's wrong with you?"

"It's Donnie. I think he's going nuts. Did you hear that last prayer?"

"No, but I'm sure Pat did. She's supposed to supervise his prayers."

"She left before he prayed this one. It's about an adventure. I tell you he—"

"Oh, forget it. I'm sure he—"

"Listen, when you put a new petition in the Lord's Prayer it's serious, and Donnie has just done that. He wants an adventure."

"But he and Granny just had a dried-apple adventure."

"He doesn't consider that an adventure. It was too tame."

"It was wild enough to strike a tree in two. Say, I'm hungry. Let's go downstairs and find something to eat. That leftover sausage we had for supper makes great sandwiches if you put mustard and pickles on it. And there is a bowl of Granny's canned peaches and—"

Pat knocked at the door and stuck her head inside. "If you guys have any idea of getting something to eat, skip it. I want that sausage for my lunch sandwich. Besides, you'll disturb Dad, who is reading. Also, you'll wake up Donnie who is no doubt dreaming about an adventure he just got through planning for God to give him."

She closed the door before the two boys could give her an answer.

"Well, that's that," Jeff said, searching for a few leftover mints he had put in his jean pockets at noon.

Kurt thumped the table. "What do you say? Shall we cure Donnie of this mental sickness about adventure?"

Jeff had started to unlace his tennis shoes, but he stopped and looked up curiously. "How can we do that?"

"Let's *give* him an adventure, and maybe *that* will cure him."

"How can you give anyone an adventure?" Jeff asked in a disgusted voice. "What do you have in your so-called mind?"

Suddenly Kurt was excited and jumped up and began to walk back and forth.

"We'll do a little kidnapping."

"Who—Dad? Granny? Pat? or Donnie himself?"

"Poochie. Just for a little while—but long enough to make Donnie realize that an adventure can be scary."

Jeff was interested enough to stop taking off his shoes and socks. "Go on," he said.

"We'll hide Poochie—see. And then we'll leave a note on his doghouse, asking for some money—maybe like five bucks. Donnie ought to have that much in his bank."

"Oh, come on—even Poochie could see through that dumb idea."

"Listen. We'll have a note that will say that if Donnie talks to the police his dog will be killed. Isn't that what real kidnappers say?"

"You think Donnie will like that adventure?" Jeff asked doubtfully.

"No one likes them while they are going on. Besides, he wants something horrible. Think what fun he'll have telling about it afterward."

"I don't think Mom or Dad would be too happy about us scaring Donnie about his pet."

"Mom's having her own adventure in San Francisco, and Dad will see through the whole thing as a joke. Besides, we'll get the dog back before Donnie gets too upset. I'll bet it will shut up his adventure-wishing."

Kurt pulled a sheet of paper from his notebook. He crumpled it and smudged it with a dirty eraser. Then he began to print.

Jeff read aloud over his brother's shoulder.

"If you want your dog back, put five dollars (change or bills) under the flat rock by the spring. Your dog will then be set free. If you tell the police—or anyone else—your dog will be *killed.*"

Jeff shook his head. "It sure sounds phony to me, but I guess Donnie will believe it. He

almost believes in Easter Bunny. You don't think he'll recognize your handwriting?"

"Come on, Jeff. He's only in the first grade. He wouldn't recognize his *own* hand-writing. Boy, will he love it—when it's over," Kurt chuckled as he read the note again.

"Where will we hide Poochie?"

"Over at Granny's, and it will have to be tonight and tomorrow, because Sam is in Chicago visiting his dad, and Granny is sleeping downstairs while Mom is gone. We'll get that long leash we have hanging in the barn and put Poochie on it, so he can be free to run up and down Granny's clothesline."

"We'll put out a pan of fresh water and a bone to chew on. Even if he does howl—which he will—we won't hear him way down here," Jeff said.

"What say? Shall we do it?" Kurt asked eagerly.

Jeff went first and tiptoed past Pat's door and Donnie's. He got down silently, because he skipped the squeeky step—and also because the Boston Pops was playing something with drums and brass going crazy. Jeff peeped in the front room and saw his dad dozing, with his chin on his chest and a *National Geographic* on his lap.

When he got to the dog pen, Poochie was happy to see him and didn't mind one bit being fastened to the long leash. The two of them walked up the hill toward Granny's house.

Little wild animals rustled in the roadside brush, and Poochie strained at the leash to go and chase them.

It was a beautiful night for a kidnapping. The moon was bright, and the air was sweet and cool. Jeff knew they wouldn't have thought of the kidnapping had it been stormy.

Soon Kurt caught up with them. "Isn't this fun?" he asked.

"I guess it's more of an adventure for us than it will be for Donnie. If Dad should look in our room and find us gone, we'll be in for it."

"He won't. Say, we aren't actually doing anything bad, are we?" Kurt asked.

"You can't say it's good either. All it will cost is a few hours of worry for Donnie."

"It's to teach him how important a nice easy home life we have. He doesn't need an adventure."

Jeff looked at his brother critically. "You know, Kurt, if you used all your brains for studying instead of stuff like this, you'd raise your grade to a B average."

"You want to stop, so let's stop," Kurt said angrily. We're not doing something criminal. It's just a little experience we are doing. Donnie should be praying for the right things."

"Is that *really* why we're doing it?" Jeff said uncertainly.

Kurt looked away from his brother. "Here we are. Want to go back home with Poochie?"

He dug in his pocket and pulled out a huge knuckle bone. "This ought to be fun for Poochie half the night."

"Tomorrow's vegetable soup," Jeff said, then shrugged. "Well, I'm not crazy about vegetable soup anyway." He went to fill a pan with fresh water and spread a rug under the line.

Kurt fastened the leash to the clothes line, both boys patted the dog lovingly and started back toward home. Poochie paid no attention to them, and they could hear him gnawing at the bone as they walked far down the hill.

They were relieved when they saw that their house was dark and knew that their father had done to bed. All the doors were locked, but the old oak tree was easily climbed as it had been many times before. They had no trouble climbing into their own room.

Jeff took a long breath as he pulled off his jeans. "At least Poochie is having an adventure. I can't say I'm too happy about the whole thing. I feel like a real kidnapper—an honest-to-goodness one."

"There are no honest ones. I hope that Donnie is a good-enough reader to figure out that note, or else he might take it to Dad to read."

"Or, he might take it to Pat. I've half a mind to jog back to Granny's and bring back the dog and tear up the note."

"If you do, you're going alone." Kurt left for the bathroom, where he turned on the shower.

Jeff sank wearily on his bed. "The trouble with me is that I haven't the guts to be good and the spunk to be bad."

CHAPTER 4

The two older Haley boys were awakened the next morning by Donnie coming barefooted into their room. He had on pajamas and his feet were wet and a little muddy. He had a puzzled frown on his pale face and in his hand was the ransom note.

He came over to Jeff's bed and held the note in front of his brother's closed eyes.

"I can read most of this but what does it mean? Poochie isn't in his house and the pen-gate was open. What does—"

"Ask Kurt, I'm still asleep," Jeff said refusing to open his eyes.

Kurt read the note aloud to his little brother. "This is serious, kid. Someone has kidnapped Poochie. You are not to tell anyone. You must put five dollars under that big flat rock by the spring."

Jeff opened one eye but closed it again quickly when he saw his brother's pale, worried face.

"Oh, my poor, poor dog," Donnie sobbed.

"Have you got five dollars?" Kurt asked.

Jeff opened both eyes and sat up. "If you

haven't, I'll help you. I've been saving for a transistor."

"I don't know, I haven't counted. I'll be back." Donnie stopped at the door and whispered. "Don't tell anyone or they'll kill my dog." The door closed softly.

"I feel like a heel," Jeff said.

"I feel like a heel too, but I'm not going to back away now."

But neither of the boys could go back to sleep, although it was still very early. Donnie came back into the room carrying his big fat piggy bank. He sat down at the boys' study table and began shaking out dimes and quarters and nickels and stacking them carefully.

"Help me count it, please," he begged and Jeff and Kurt got up, looking ashamed and unhappy.

"Get me an envelope and I'll put the money in it as I count," Kurt said.

Donnie tiptoed out of the room.

"Let's tell him. I can't stand this," Jeff said miserably, but Kurt only had time to shake his head before Donnie was back in the room with a slightly used envelope.

"You have 47 cents left over. You want me to go down to the flat rock with you?" Kurt asked.

Donnie got even more white and sick looking. "Oh, *no*! They'd kill my dog right away if they thought I'd told anyone. My poor dog has

43

never been kidnapped before, he might be scared to death. I hope they gave him a breakfast."

"I'm sure they won't hurt him," Jeff felt like a hypocrite and hated himself and Kurt for ever thinking up anything so cruel.

Donnie left with the envelope. He paused at the door. "The poor pup doesn't even know what kidnapping is. I hope they don't tell him."

Kurt and Jeff looked out of their window and saw the little boy disappear in the heavy foliage that almost hid the path down to the spring.

Jeff began dressing in a hurry. "I'm going up and untie that dog this minute. Somehow that trick seems much worse this morning than it did last night."

"I'll go with you," Kurt said, pulling on a T-shirt.

"No, you stay here and comfort that poor kid until his dog comes running home."

"I hear Granny in the kitchen. Guess Pop had an early breakfast and left, because his car is gone. I'll wait for Donnie in the back yard."

Jeff went out the front door quietly and hurried up the road. The air was heavy and damp and in the hollows of the hills there were milky bowls of fog.

Jeff was so anxious to get Poochie that he broke into a run up the hill. Granny's house looked cozy, wrapped in mist. Jeff hurried to the back yard.

But he stopped short when he got there. The line was heavy with sparkling dewdrops. The dish had been turned over, and the rug was rumpled and damp, with a part of a chewed bone on it.

But the long leash hung empty. There was no dog. The leash was not torn or pried open. It must have been opened neatly and the dog released.

Cold fear wormed itself inside Jeff's stomach, and he began calling the dog. His voice echoed back from the hill beyond the meadow, but there were no answering barks.

"Hey, what's all the yelling about? Where's Poochie?" Kurt came up breathless from his dash up the hill. "Donnie put the money under the rock and is sitting on the front porch waiting for his dog. He didn't want me around for fear the dog would not be released."

"The dog's gone," Jeff said, hoarse from his frantic calling.

"Gone! But he can't be." Kurt went over and examined the clasp. "There's nothing wrong with this. He *couldn't* have gotten loose by himself. I made a triple check to be sure it was fastened."

"He's gone. And the only way he could be gone is if someone unfastened the clip. You don't think that maybe Dad could—" Jeff stopped in horror.

"We'd know about it by now. Besides, the

dog pen is on the other side of the house from where Dad parks his car. Why should he go over there?"

"If someone had unfastened him, Poochie would have dashed home like crazy."

"I know. That's what scares me. But who would want to steal a half-grown, mixed-up-breed dog?"

"I don't know. I *do* know that Poochie is such a friendly dog he'd go with the devil himself—even if he had to leave a half-chewed bone." Jeff took the leash off the clothes line. "There's nothing left to do but tell Dad."

"Oh, rats! I can just imagine what *he* will—" Kurt broke off, his eyes on the road coming from town. Both boys stood frozen when they saw that it was a police car and that it was slowing down.

The car slowed to a stop at Granny's house. The uniformed man got out a book and checked the mailbox number. Then he turned off the motor and got out of the car.

Jeff called in a shaky voice. "No one's home here."

The man turned, then came around to where they stood. His keen eyes took in the clothes line, the leash, and the rug.

"I understand a dog was kidnapped from here last night," he said, checking his notebook.

"Not really," Kurt said nervously. "You

see the dog belonged to our kid brother and we—"

The officer glanced at his book. "Are you Kurt and Jeffrey Haley?"

The boys nodded. They were trying their best to act calm and innocent.

"I'll have to take you in for questioning. Even kidnapping an animal is—"

Kurt was so nervous he broke in quickly, "But it was just a joke. You see our little brother has been—"

The officer was reading his notebook. "You see we have a note that has been identified as one of your handwritings."

"Mine," Kurt said bravely. "Mr. Officer, we were honestly just playing a joke on our kid brother."

"I'm sorry, kid. You'll have to tell someone beside me. I'm to bring you in. Jump in the car, boys."

Jeff and Kurt followed the officer around the house and jumped in the back seat when the man opened the door.

"Jokes can turn out to be bad news, kids," the man said as he got in the front seat.

Jeff and Kurt did not look at each other. With eyes glazed with dread they watched the familiar scenery fly by. It was like a horrible nightmare. They were in a *police car*. No doubt they were going to the police station.

The little town seemed still to be dozing.

There were hardly any cars or people around. Fog tipped the bluffs across the river, and everything seemed unreal.

Yes, the car was headed toward the police station. Jeff was glad he hadn't had any breakfast because he felt sick. The car stopped in front of the station, and the driver came to open the door for the two boys to slink out. If they hadn't been so terrified they could have seen a twinkle in the officer's eyes.

A man sat at a big desk. He looked up and motioned the officer toward a closed door. The policeman went over to open it and ushered the boys inside, then backed out and closed the door.

"Dad!" both boys gasped as they saw their father in the chair on the other side of the desk.

"Sit down," he said sternly and Jeff and Kurt sat on the edge of the chairs, neither feeling any relief that the man behind the desk was their own father.

"Now, will you please explain this to me."

Kurt cleared his throat. "It was just a little joke, Dad. Donnie had this crazy idea that he was underprivileged because he wasn't having any adventures, so we thought we'd give him one."

"It was no little joke. It was a mean trick. You both know how much your little brother loves his dog."

"We intended giving the dog back right away, and his money too," Jeff ventured.

"To deliberately cause *anyone* anxiety and pain for even ten minutes is inexcusable. I really didn't think either of you would do such a thing."

The boys were silent.

"I got up early and happened to see the note. Anyone but a trusting six-year old would have figured out what was going on. It was stupid—besides being mean. I asked the officer to pick you up after I took Poochie home. I figured a few minutes of feeling you were on the wrong side of the law would teach you something."

"We're sorry, sir. When we saw that Poochie was gone, we felt awful, didn't we, Jeff?"

"Yes, sir. I guess we didn't realize how mean it was until we saw Donnie this morning."

"You could have stopped the whole thing right there."

Neither boy could answer that.

"You are going home now—walking— and then talking with your brother. I haven't decided yet what privileges will be taken away from both of you for a while—also a few jobs added. Now, I have to go to my office."

The man at the desk didn't look up and Kurt and Jeff slunk out of the police station as if they were the very lowest of crooks.

Donnie was sitting on the front steps with his arm around his dog.

Pat came out and listened to the boys as they apologized to Donnie.

"Of all the lousy tricks," she cried.

Donnie looked up at the boys.

"You have to apologize to Poochie, too. After all, he has feelings and he doesn't like to be kidnapped and tied to a clothesline all night."

"But we gave him a big meaty bone," Kurt protested.

"So that's where that bone went. I thought someone got so hungry last night that they stole a bone," Granny said, coming to the door.

"Go on—tell Poochie you're sorry,"

Kurt hesitated but Jeff went over to the dog and held out his hand. Poochie had been trained to shake hands and he gladly shook hands with Jeff.

"I'm sorry, Poochie."

"If he could talk he'd tell you both that he'll never believe you again." Donnie said with dignity. "Now, go on, Kurt—it's your turn."

Pat went inside, and she and Granny ran to the kitchen, trying to smother their laughter. It was funny enough to see Jeff apologizing to a dog and shaking his paw, but to watch stiff-necked Kurt do the same thing was too much.

"I hope that'll teach them," Pat said, wiping tears of laughter on her shirttail.

CHAPTER 5

The sewing machine hummed and the transistor radio pounded out the kind of old-fashioned music his mother and dad loved.

Donnie shouted to be heard above the noise.

"You never told us what your adventure was, Mom," Donnie asked for the third time.

Mrs. Haley shut off the machine and turned down the radio. "I did tell you. The entire trip was a lovely, delightful adventure. I loved every minute of it even if I did get lonesome for my family."

"But adventures aren't supposed to be 'lovely'! They are scary and you never know what's going to happen next—and stuff like that. So, you really didn't have an adventure."

Mrs. Haley started her sewing machine, then her lips tightened and she turned to Donnie. "I'm getting a little tired of this 'adventure' business, Donnie. I thought your experience with the boys would cure you, but I see it didn't. You have a good talk with your Dad about it, will you? I'd like very much to get on with this dress I'm making for Pat. Will you *please* go

51

outside for a while and amuse yourself playing games with your dog."

The hum of the sewing machine seemed louder than ever, and the music from the small radio got on Donnie's nerves. He wished that grown-ups would realize that kids had nerves too and that you didn't have to be old to get cross about things. He went outside, but he closed the door softly after him.

It was a hot summer afternoon, but when Donnie got out on the front porch he found a sweet-smelling breeze blowing over the meadows. He realized that he loved the outdoor smells and noises. A humming bird fluttered over the four-o'clocks, and hundreds of grasshoppers were singing solos at the same time. Back in the woods a mockingbird was making fun of the chickens and cackling like he'd just layed an egg.

Jeff and Kurt had cut the grass that morning, and it was so short that Donnie saw Bigblack slithering across the front lawn. Bigblack was a snake that lived in a hole near the barn. He was a very friendly snake and no doubt knew that he could feel safe because no Haly killed harmless snakes.

Donnie remembered the first time they had become acquainted with Bigblack. Pat was taking a bath in the downstairs bathroom, and when she looked out of the window she saw a big long black snake curled around a limb of the big oak by the window. It was staring curiously at Pat—or she thought it was.

Donnie laughed out loud when he remembered how Pat had screamed and ran dripping through the house with only a beach towel around her middle.

"He's looking at me! he's looking at me!" she had screeched.

But Pat had gotten used to Bigblack taking his afternoon rest period staring in the bathroom window.

The telephone ringing brought Donnie back to the present and he jumped up to answer it. He knew that his mother would never hear it ringing with the sewing machine and the transistor going.

When Donnie lifted the receiver and said hello, he heard heavy breathing like someone trying to catch his breath.

"Who is this?" Donnie asked.

"It's me, Kurt. You and Mom both inside the house?"

Donnie liked to try the crazy-talk that Jeff, Kurt, and Sam always used.

"No, I'm on top of the telephone post and Mom is outside standing on her head on the bagswing."

"Cut out the smart talk and listen to me. This is serious. Are you listening?"

"Yes."

"Where's Poochie?"

"I guess he's down under the willow, where he always goes on hot afternoons. Why?"

"Go right down and get him this very minute. Lock him in the basement. You hear? And then you and Mom don't dare to step outside."

Donnie felt a surge of excitement tingling from his toes to his head but he wasn't going to let his brother know that. They weren't going to fool him again.

"Why? Is there another kidnapper out there?"

"Please *listen,* Donnie. This is no joke. It could be a life and death matter."

"Well, tell me, although I'm not sure I'll believe you—not after—"

Donnie could hear talking. One voice sounded like Sam. Jeff too was there because his voice went up high like a girl's when he got nervous.

Donnie heard Kurt say to someone, "Say, mister, is that gun really loaded?"

"A gun!" Donnie shouted, and someone picked up the telephone. It was Jeff.

"We're going with the men now," Jeff said, as if he thought Donnie knew all about what was going on. "You do what Kurt said. Tell Mom we've already called Pat and she's on her way home. She should be there in a few minutes."

"But—" Donnie shouted.

The phone went dead, and Donnie put down the receiver. Were those smart brothers of his pulling another dumb joke? They had sounded serious—but then that kidnap note had sounded serious too. Yet something inside him kept reminding him how scared the boys had sounded. They weren't that good at acting. If only he knew from where the boys had called he could check back.

A door opened upstairs, and Mrs. Haley called.

"What are you yelling about, Donnie? Who was that on the phone?"

"Kurt and Jeff, and I'm supposed to get the dog in, and you and I are not supposed to step outdoors—not even one foot—it's life and death."

"Another adventure I suppose. Those boys! I'm thoroughly sick of the word. I'm not wild about Poochie in the basement, but go get him if you're lonesome."

The sewing room door closed. What was wrong with grown-ups? They got all excited about things that really weren't important, like forgetting to brush teeth or putting on clean socks or picking your nose in church, but when a life-and-death thing came up they just got cross and went on like nothing was going to happen.

Maybe nothing *was* going to happen.

But just to be sure, he'd better get Poochie this very minute. No doubt the boys were planning an adventure, and he wished he could be in on it. But, no, there he was stuck at home with his Mom, and his dog, and Bigblack.

He ran down to the back yard and parted the heavy, drooping branches of the big willow tree. There was the nice soft dust-hole that Poochie had made but Poochie was not in it. Where could that dog be? He might have gone down to the river for a cooling dip.

There was nothing he could do but make a quick run to the river and get that little dickens. Donnie was afraid not to do what Kurt had told him. Maybe there was some awful germ or gas floating that way—perhaps a murderer had escaped from the prison. He should have told his mother where he was going. No. He'd be back home with his dog in a few minutes. They both were very fast runners.

He broke into a run as he got on the path to the river. He sniffed the air. But poison might not smell. He heard a rustle in the brush beside the path and stopped to call his dog. But Poochie did not come bounding out. He was worried. His dog *always* came when his master called—especially when it was late afternoon and just about feeding time.

But when Donnie got to the river he saw no sign of his pup. Nor were there any wet tracks to show where Poochie had climbed the bank from a cool dip.

Donnie called and called, but there was

no sign of his dog. There was only one other place that Poochie went without his master, and that was up to Granny's house.

The more Donnie thought about what Kurt and Jeff had said, the more excitement built up inside him. Of course the boys could be playing one of their dumb jokes again, but somehow he didn't think they were. He knew that their dad had made it plain what he thought about *that*. This time they might really be telling the truth. Something might be going on that was dangerous.

The woods suddenly seemed scary. He decided he'd better go to the open road. He could also make much faster time that way. While he headed for the fence by the road, he realized that he was running away from something he knew nothing about. It was *much* worse than knowing!

He had barely climbed the fence and jumped to the road, when he heard men's voices. He sank back into the bushes in the ditch. Three men walked around the curve in the road. They looked pale and worried.

All three of them carried guns!

Something *was* happening—or going to happen. It wasn't poisonous gas either. No one carried a gun for that.

Through the thick branches of the bushes Donnie stared at the men. Two of them he didn't know but one was a farmer that lived near town and did part-time work at his school. His name was Higgins, and another custodian at the school had called him a loud-mouth. But Mr. Higgins was talking softly, as if he was scared. He also looked back, right, left, and everyplace but up, as though he knew something was near—something bad. Donnie could not hear what he was saying but they were coming nearer.

Donnie held his breath. He had the feeling that if he moved suddenly, all three men would fire at him and he would go down like a cowboy in a western movie.

"When was it you first saw him?" the tall thin man with a wart on his nose asked.

"This morning about five," Mr. Higgins said softly, still looking around in a frightened way, "I was out doing my milking before breakfast. It was just getting light and I saw him in the south pasture. I noticed something funny in his walk."

"Was he running?" the wart-man asked.

"No, that's what made me look at him again. He was just sort of trotting. He was moving his head from side to side. The way he acted I *knew*. I dropped my cans and headed for the house and for my gun."

The third man began looking around too and Donnie was sure his own lungs would burst right out of his chest if he didn't take a deep breath.

The three men were right in front of Donnie's hiding place.

"Go on—why didn't you shoot him right then while you had a chance?" the wart-man asked.

"My kid used my gun in the school play last spring and didn't put it back where it belonged. Also, I had to find the—"

The third man muttered something that made Mr. Higgins mad.

"I had to wake the kid to find out what he'd done with the gun. Then I had to load it."

"By that time I guess he was long gone," the wart-man said with disgust.

"When I got outside there was no sign of him. That's when I called the state troopers, and then I called you. My kid, without my permission, called a bunch of big boys, and I told them to watch the road right outside our house and fields."

"How about your cattle?"

"I told my wife to—" they were past Donnie, and he could no longer hear what was being said. But he was no longer in doubt that someone dangerous was out prowling around near to where he was.

As soon as the men were around the next turn he jumped out from the bushes and ran as fast as he could up the road to Granny's house. He had no breath left to call his dog. But he was scared. He knew this was no half-joke his brothers were playing.

The first thing he would do would be to warn Granny, and he would ask her if she'd seen Poochie. A sudden knife-like cut of fear sliced through him when he remembered that he had not convinced his mother that some sort of bad thing was happening. He made up his mind to call her from Granny's house.

The little white cottage came into view. How cheerful it looked in the rays of the golden afternoon sun. There was no sign of his dog however. Granny never locked her door during the daytime, so Donnie went into the kitchen.

Donnie called but no one answered. Granny's household pet, Graycat, sat in the rocker licking her paws as the chair swayed back and forth. It looked so peaceful—but it wasn't.

The phone rang and Donnie goose-pimpled. He was afraid to answer it and afraid not to. But it kept ringing, and he lifted the receiver and said a very faint hello.

"Oh, darling, thank God you are there. I was so worried. You should have told me you were going to Granny's."

"I didn't know it. But I couldn't find Poochie and—Mom, why are you so worried?"

His mother's voice was tight like a rubber on a slingshot stretched to shoot. "Donnie, listen carefully. This is terribly important.

There is a mad dog loose and roaming around our neighborhood."

"Mad?"

"Listen!" I beg you to listen, darling. This dog has a terrible sickness called rabies. If he bites another dog or a person *they* could get the sickness. It's a horrible sickness and can kill. Understand?"

Donnie tried to hold the receiver steady, so he wouldn't miss a word.

His mother went on, talking slowly and beating out each word as though she was hammering them into his brain. "You *must* stay inside Granny's house and keep your dog *inside* with you. Granny won't be home. She's in town. Now, I'll come for you as soon as I know it's safe and someone is here to take me. Turn on the radio. They just said that they are certain the dog is around *here.*"

"But—" Donnie tried to keep his teeth from that awful clattering noise, so he could talk. He tried again. "But, Poochie—"

His mother seemed to have turned her head. "O, thank heavens, here is Pat. I know the boys are safe with the police, and dad is in his office. Now, remember, *do not leave the house* until you hear from me."

Donnie heard the sob in his mother's voice as the phone went dead. He knew she was hugging his sister in her relief that Pat was home. He wished she was hugging *him.* He felt so alone without a single member of his family to protect or advise him. Why, he didn't even have his dog.

His dog!

He ran out the kitchen door to Granny's screened porch. Far beyond Granny's fenced-in yard, chasing something in the tall meadow-grass he saw the top of Poochie's head. Poochie was bounding high in the weeds, joyously chasing some little wild animal.

He tried to steady himself. All he had to do was get his dog inside Granny's fenced-in yard and close the gate. Then they would be safe. But when Donnie glanced down the drive-way, he saw that the wide gate at the end of the yard was open. When Granny went somewhere in her little old car she never closed the gate. The yard was not safe—yet.

What should he do first? Close the gate or get Poochie inside the yard? He'd better get his dog. Poochie was such a playful pup. He tried to yell, but something was wrong with his throat. It was dry with fear. He swallowed hard and stood on the steps outside the porch and called his dog with a shrill terror-filled voice.

Donnie could barely see his dog's head but Poochie heard his master's voice and stopped short, his ears up. Donnie called again and Poochie gave a joyful bark and began a leaping run toward the house.

Ah! his dog would soon be safe inside the house. Thank you, God—O, thanks.

But the relief had hardly flooded over him, when out of the corner of his eye he saw a movement, and he turned and saw something move in the driveway. An animal moving slowly but steadily toward the house.

He knew instantly! It was the sick dog and never again as long as he lived would he ever forget that sight.

It was a big dog and strange to Donnie. It looked to him as if the head was enlarged. The poor creature's eyes were filmed and his head moved from side to side as if he were suffering. Foam dribbled from its mouth.

And over beyond the yard fence Poochie was bouncing joyfully toward his little master. Poochie would jump the low fence to get to Donnie. He would be in the path of the mad dog.

The sick animal had just started up the long driveway. If Donnie ran fast, he could meet Poochie and grab his collar and pull him inside the screened porch and into the house. He dared not wait because Poochie would investigate any strange animal. Donnie had seen it happen too often.

Poochie had just jumped the low fence and had only a little way to go to get to the driveway.

Donnie flew down the steps and across

the driveway. His heart was thumping so hard it hurt.

He rushed toward his dog but was stunned when Poochie suddenly stopped short. His hair bristled and he quivered, looking in the direction of the driveway. Poochie sensed something awful was there.

Donnie grabbed the collar of his dog and pulled so frantically that he almost choked him, but Poochie stood frozen. Donnie knew he had no way to pull his dog across the driveway. He pulled and yanked and then turned to see how far up the sick dog had come.

They were cut off from the house! In no way could they make it anymore. The dog was between them and the doorway to the porch.

Donnie had no idea what a mad dog would do. Would he chase someone? All that the boy was sure of was that he and his pup were directly in the path of the dangerous creature. Donnie looked around. Where could they go to be safe?

Directly in back of them was Granny's fruit cellar. The flat doors were opened, because Granny evidently wanted to air out the damp, cellar-like place.

Without more thinking, Donnie gave a hard yank at Poochie's collar and started down the damp rock cellar steps. Poochie, surprised, lost his balance and rolled down the steps. It gave Donnie time to reach up and pull the one door closed above his head. He reached for the other door and found himself staring close to the suffering eyes of the mad dog. He slammed the door shut and he and Poochie were in darkness. There was a small crack in one of the doors that let in enough light to show Poochie on his feet, but making no effort to climb the damp steps. Instead he whimpered and crowded closer to his master.

Donnie held him tightly. His dog's warm quivering body was comforting. He realized the terror above them, and Donnie breathed a prayer of thanks. They were safe. Soon some searchers would find the dog, and they could get outside again.

Donnie stared at the crack of light. It made him uneasy. The cellar doors were very, very old and worn—with any weight at all they could crash in. Was the dog on the doors? The driveway ended at the back porch steps, which were directly across from the cellar.

Was that a noise of heavy breathing?

"God," Donnie said out loud. "Please forgive me. I'm truly sorry I bothered you about adventures. Please, help us and I'll behave and be happy just going to school and coming home every day. I'll be happy—I *promise* to be happy." He finished with a sob and tears dripped on Poochie's head.

Then suddenly there was a shot—and then another one. Right after the shots there was a cheerful sound of voices. They were calling. Yes, they were calling him. It surely must be safe to open the cellar doors.

He climbed up the slippery steps, still keeping a tight hold on Poochie's collar. There was no longer a crack of light from the old door. When Donnie slowly lifted the door, he saw that it was beginning to get dark. He saw a group of people standing in a circle gazing down at something lying on the ground. It was the dead dog.

Around the house came his family with Sam and Granny. He opened the cellar door wide and ran up the rest of the steps.

"I'm here," he shouted.

"Oh, darling, I'm so thankful," his mother was crying, and his dad hugged him so hard that Donnie could hardly breathe.

"I'll hold the dog. We don't want him to get near that animal even if it is dead. They'll take him away now," Kurt said, getting a firm grip on Poochie.

"Why the cellar?" Pat asked, gazing down at the dark damp hole.

"Because that sick dog blocked our way to the house. Granny, thanks for leaving those doors open."

"Thank God," even Granny was trembling, but she tried to hide it.

"I was in town when they said they were sure they had the dog cornered right here. I couldn't believe the announcer on the radio," she said. Greycat came and rubbed against Granny's skirt, and she picked it up and petted it.

"I saw the dog coming. I *saw* him. I'll never, never forget that awful-looking dog. Oh, Dad, he was so sick. I'll be afraid to close my eyes tonight, because I'll keep seeing him."

"No you won't," his mother said. "After you say your prayers you'll have a nice peaceful sleep."

"What made him get the sickness?" Donnie asked as they watched some men lift the big sack, with the dog in it, to a truck."

"Wild animals sometimes can bite dogs and pass on the sickness. That's why we can't take chances with Poochie in the woods for a while. I'm proud of you, Donnie. You showed a lot of courage and good sense," his father said.

Later that evening as the entire family sat in front of the big fireplace and munched popcorn, Donnie wondered at how wonderful it felt just to be safe in his own house with all his family.

Even Poochie must have felt that way because he went around to everyone offering his paw in a friendly handshake.

Donnie thought to himself. "I'll never, never bother God with a dumb prayer again."

Poochie came to shake his hand.